I0813567

MY FAVORITE DOG

DALMATIANS

by Jim Whiting
Dog Expert: Beth Adelman, MS
Former editor, *American Kennel Club Gazette*

Kaleidoscope
Minneapolis, MN

The Quest for Discovery Never Ends

This edition first published in 2021 by Kaleidoscope Publishing, Inc.

For information regarding permission, write to
Kaleidoscope Publishing, Inc.
6012 Blue Circle Drive
Minnetonka, MN 55343

Library of Congress Control Number
2020936237

ISBN
978-1-64519-440-8 (library bound)
978-1-64519-452-1 (ebook)

Printed in the United States of America.

FIND ME IF YOU CAN!

Bigfoot lurks within one of the images in this book. It's up to you to find him!

TABLE OF **CONTENTS**

Introduction

Here Comes a Dalmatian!

Mario had always wanted a dog. His parents promised he could have one for his eighth birthday. He would be old enough to take good care of it.

Today was the big day! Before his friends came over for cake and ice cream, he was going to get his new puppy.

He always knew what he wanted. A Dalmatian! Mario's favorite movie ever was *101 Dalmatians*. He watched it over and over.

They arrived at the **breeder**. The puppies stayed in a special room. They all scurried to meet Mario. They were all so cute and lively! Mario took a long time to decide. Finally, he pointed to one. "That's Patch," he said. It was the name of a puppy in the movie.

As they drove home, Mario cuddled Patch in his lap. He could hardly wait to show him to his friends!

FUN FACT
Dalmatians have had many nicknames, including Fire Dog, Carriage Dog, and Plum Pudding Dog!

Chapter 1
The Story of Dalmatians

Mario had read a lot about Dalmatians. He learned that the breed is named for Dalmatia. That is a part of Croatia in southern Europe.

Dalmatians had a very special job. They get along very well with horses, so they trotted beside horse-drawn coaches. They chased off stray dogs. They guarded the coaches when they stopped. They even warned when robbers were just ahead! Dalmatians needed a lot of **endurance** to keep up with the horses for hour after hour. They were the **marathoners** of the dog family!

FUN FACT

President George Washington liked to breed Dalmatians. His favorite was named Madame Moose.

For many years, horses pulled fire engines. Dalmatians ran ahead to clear the way. Then they stayed with the horses. That calmed them while the firemen did their job. Firefighters today use powerful trucks. Many of them keep Dalmatians as **mascots** in their firehouses.

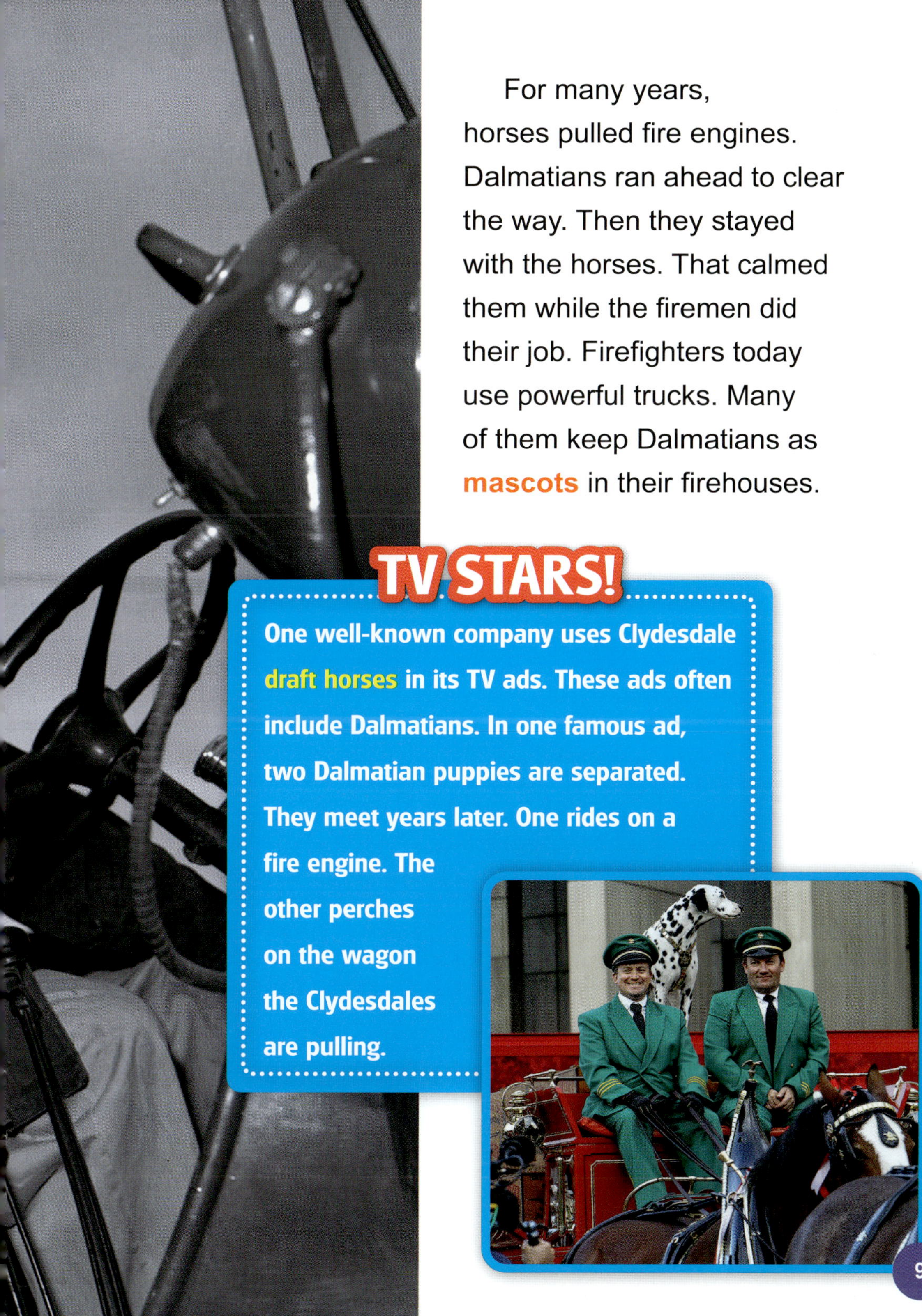

TV STARS!

One well-known company uses Clydesdale **draft horses** in its TV ads. These ads often include Dalmatians. In one famous ad, two Dalmatian puppies are separated. They meet years later. One rides on a fire engine. The other perches on the wagon the Clydesdales are pulling.

In 1961, Disney Productions released the movie *101 Dalmatians*. It is based on a book by British author Dodie Smith. Fashion designer Cruella de Vil kidnaps a litter of Dalmatian puppies. She wants to make fur coats from their hair. The puppies' parents are Pongo and Perdita. They set out to save them. They have many adventures along the way. Finally, they find their puppies. They also find many other Dalmatian puppies that Cruella has taken. Pongo and Perdita rescue all 101 of them! The film made Dalmatians popular.

A **sequel** called *102 Dalmatians* was released in 2000. Another sequel is *Cruella*. It will be released in 2021.

WHERE DALMATIANS COME FROM

NORWAY

SCOTLAND

North Sea

IRELAND

ENGLAND

GERMANY

SLOVENIA

Atlantic Ocean

FRANCE

CROATIA

ITALY

SPAIN

Dalmatia, Croatia

N
W
E
S

The AKC was founded in 1884. It first registered Dalmatians four years later.

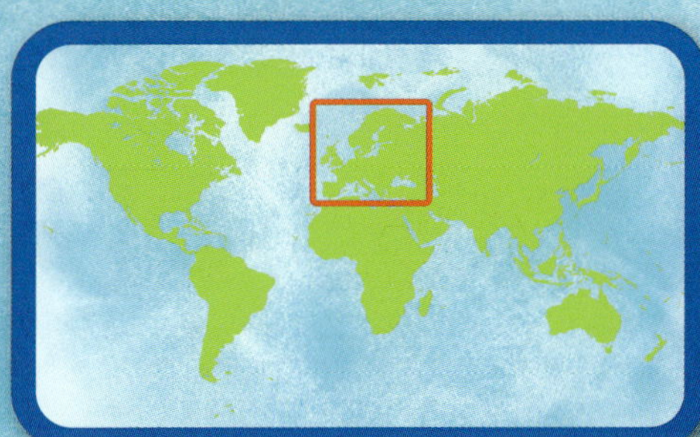

Chapter 2

Looking at a Dalmatian

The American Kennel Club (AKC) keeps track of dog breeds. The AKC puts all dogs into seven different groups. Dalmatians belong to the

This Dalmatian's coat color is called liver.

Non-Sporting Group. Many different kinds of breeds are in this group. Other dogs in the Non-Sporting Group are Boston Terriers, Bulldogs, Chow Chows, and Poodles.

All Dalmatians are white and covered with spots. These spots cover their entire bodies. The most common color of those spots is black. A shade of brown called liver is also common.

THE

DALMATIAN

MALES

HEIGHT*:
19–24 inches (48–61 cm)

WEIGHT:
45–70 lbs. (20–32 kg)

FEMALES

HEIGHT*:
19–22 inches (48–56 cm)

WEIGHT:
45–60 lbs. (20–27 kg)

**The height of a dog is measured from the top of the shoulder, not from the top of the head.*

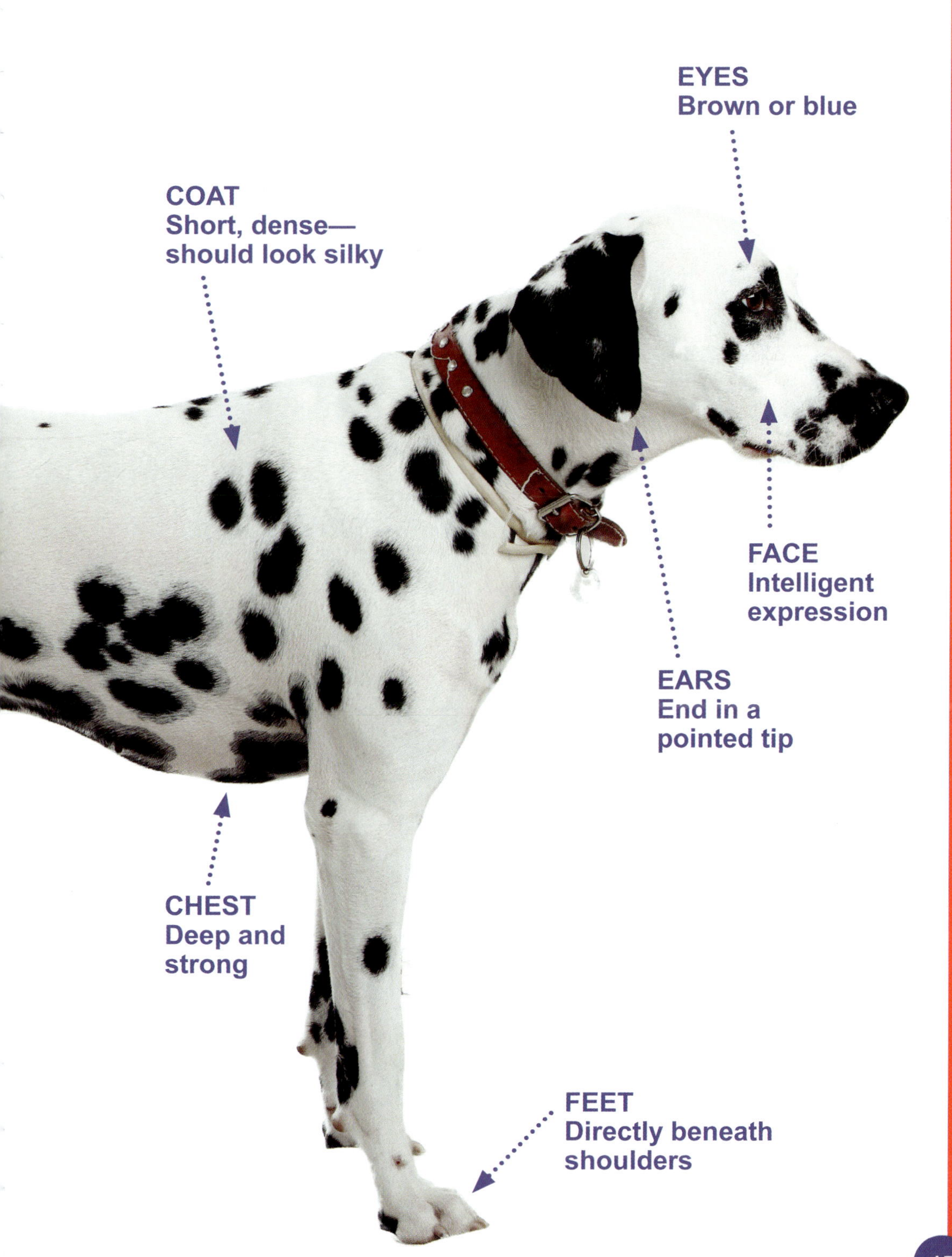
EYES
Brown or blue
COAT
Short, dense—
should look silky
FACE
Intelligent
expression
EARS
End in a
pointed tip
CHEST
Deep and
strong
FEET
Directly beneath
shoulders

Mario plays with Patch every day. They have so much fun together! The months fly by. Now Patch is fully grown. Mario wants a new adventure for his dog.

The Dalmatian Club of America sponsors road **trials**. These trials test the dog's ability to follow a horse on a long trail. The dog must not be on a leash. He must keep up a steady pace for a long time. He also has to prove that he can behave in public places.

Mario looks forward to entering these trials. He knows Patch will do very well. It will be one more way to have fun with his four-footed best friend.

Road trials are a team sport with horse, rider, and Dalmatians.

Chapter 3

Meet a Dalmatian!

Dalmatians love lots of exercise! They don't do well in tiny apartments. Mario is happy that he lives in a house with a big fenced yard. Patch can go outside and run around. He really likes it when Mario plays fetch! He romps after the ball. Then he brings it back.

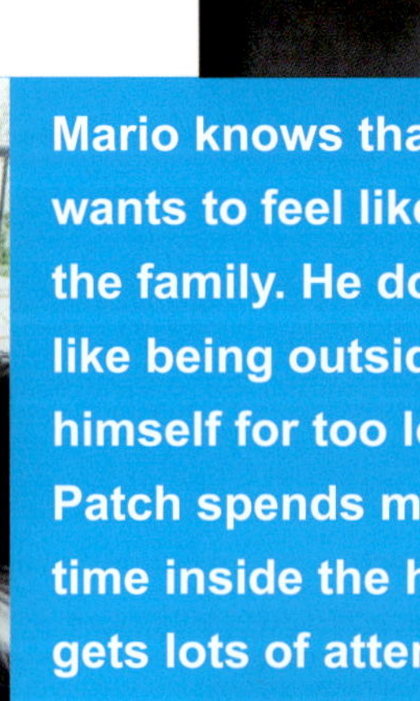

Mario knows that Patch wants to feel like part of the family. He doesn't like being outside by himself for too long. So Patch spends most of his time inside the house. He gets lots of attention.

When Patch was still a puppy, Mario began training him. Patch learned to sit, stay, roll over, and do other things.

Leash training was the next step. Mario taught Patch to walk close without pulling on the leash. Now they take walks together. That helps Patch stay healthy. Patch gets excited when he sees Mario pick up the leash. He knows he's going for another walk. He loves being outside and exploring the neighborhood.

Sometimes the family takes Patch to an off-leash dog park! He likes to play with the other dogs. Their owners tell Mario what a handsome dog Patch is.

SPOTLESS

A Dalmatian puppy is entirely white when he is born. He doesn't have any spots. Within a few weeks, darker hairs begin to replace some of the white ones. They form spots. These spots soon cover his entire body.

Chapter 4

Caring for a Dalmatian

When Mario wakes up every morning, he knows that Patch is hungry. It is important for Patch to eat the right kind of dog food. Mario asked the **veterinarian** for advice. He learned that Dalmatians have a special need. They have problems digesting **proteins**. Yet they need proteins to stay healthy. The veterinarian

Dalmatians have spots on almost every part of their bodies, including their tails. Some Dalmatians even have spots inside their mouths!

recommended food with a limited amount of high-quality protein. Fish and chicken are good choices. Giving Patch kibbles once in a while helps keep his teeth clean. Mario makes sure Patch always has plenty of water.

BATHING

Dalmatians are good at cleaning themselves. Natural oils in their coats help them shed dirt. They also have sensitive skin. Too many baths can irritate them. So Patch only needs a bath every three months or so.

Mario does other things to keep Patch healthy and happy. Dalmatians shed a lot of their fur. Mario makes sure to brush Patch every day for a minute or two. Once a week, he brushes the dog for longer. He uses grooming gloves or a brush with stiff bristles.

Patch needs his nails trimmed every six to eight weeks. Mario also gives him flea and tick treatments every three months, so nothing bites him!

Like all pets, Patch needs regular checkups by the veterinarian. The doctor looks at Patch to make sure he is healthy. He also gives him shots. Those shots keep him from getting diseases.

Mario is so happy that Patch joined his family! He takes good care of him. He plays with him. He will enjoy being with Patch for many years to come!

FUN FACT

The Dalmatian Club of America was founded in 1905. It promotes Dalmatians in the United States and around the world.

BEYOND THE BOOK

After reading the book, it's time to think about what you learned. Try the following exercises to jumpstart your ideas.

RESEARCH

FIND OUT MORE. There is so much more to find out about Dalmatians. Visit the American Kennel Club's site to research Dalmatians. Or look for a Dalmatian Club in your area. You can meet other people who love your favorite breed!

CREATE

TIME FOR ART. As you saw in the book, Dalmatians have a long history with firefighters. Read more about this history. Then get some art materials and get creative! Design a Dalmatian mascot for your local fire department. What gear will it wear? What sort of face will it have? How can you make it look friendly for kids?

DISCOVER

LOTS OF BREEDS. This book is about your favorite dog breed. But there are hundreds more around the world. Visit the AKC site or those of other dog organizations. What other breeds can you discover? Which breeds are related to your favorite? What is the most interesting new breed you have discovered?

GROW

HELP OUT! Animal shelters can be great places to volunteer. Contact a shelter near you and find out if you can help. Or can your family donate food or gear to help rescue dogs? Find out why dogs end up in shelters. Is there anything you can do to help them find homes?

Visit www.ninjaresearcher.com/4408 to learn how to take your research skills and book report writing to the next level!

RESEARCH

SEARCH LIKE A PRO

Learn about how to use search engines to find useful websites.

FACT OR FAKE?

Discover how you can tell a trusted website from an untrustworthy resource.

TEXT DETECTIVE

Explore how to zero in on the information you need most.

SHOW YOUR WORK

Research responsibly—learn how to cite sources.

WRITE

GET TO THE POINT

Learn how to express your main ideas.

PLAN OF ATTACK

Learn prewriting exercises and create an outline.

DOWNLOADABLE REPORT FORMS

Further Resources

BOOKS

Klukow, Mary Ellen. *Dalmatians.* Mankato, Minn.: Amicus Publishing, 2019.

Korman, Justine. *101 Dalmatians.* New York: Golden/ Disney, 2007.

Mathea, Heidi. *Dalmatians.* North Mankato, Minn.: Checkerboard Library, 2010.

Murray, Julie. *Dalmatians.* Pinehurst, N.C.: Buddy Books, 2002.

Schuh, Mari. *Dalmatians.* Minnetonka, Minn.: Bellwether Media, 2017.

WEBSITES

Factsurfer.com gives you a safe, fun way to find more information.

1. Go to www.factsurfer.com.
2. Enter "Dalmatians" into the search box and click 🔍
3. Select your book cover to see a list of related websites.

Glossary

breeder: person who raises dogs or other animals for sale.

draft horses: large horses bred to perform work, often farm work such as plowing.

endurance: the ability to keep at something for a long time.

marathoners: people who run long distances, especially the 26.2-mile marathon.

mascot: an animal who brings good luck to a group.

proteins: substances needed for healthy bones and muscles.

sequel: a movie that continues the story of an earlier movie.

trials: tests or contests.

veterinarian: a doctor for animals.

PHOTO CREDITS

The images in this book are reproduced through the courtesy of: Alamy: Juniors Bildarchive Gmbh 6. American Kennel Club: 8. AP Images: Cheryl Senter 8B. iStock: Pedro Sanchez Sueza 17; Judy Rothchild 18; SolStock 18B; Mehmet Milmi Barcin 20; BilevichOlga 25. Newscom: Walt Disney Productions 10. Shutterstock: Eric Isselee 3; New Africa 12; RissaCar 13; Celig 14; Eudyptula 21; Susan Schmitz 22; Sergey Fatin; 23; SasPartout 24; Lisjatina 26. Peggy Ann Strupp: 16. **Cover and page 1:** Miras Wonderland/iStock. Paw prints: Maximillian Laschon/ Shutterstock.

About the Author

Jim Whiting has written more than 300 nonfiction books for kids. He lives with Vinnie, a fluffy Corgi. Vinnie is a happy dog. But he can't wag his tail. He doesn't have one!